Mohawk Valley

The Wolf Whisperer Series, Volume 3

Angeline Gallant

Published by Angeline Gallant, 2021.

This is a work of fiction. Similarities to real people, places, or events are entirely coincidental.

MOHAWK VALLEY

First edition. November 29, 2021.

Copyright © 2021 Angeline Gallant.

ISBN: 979-8201749651

Written by Angeline Gallant.

Table of Contents

Chapter 1

Chief Long Knife held Dark Star against his side as they followed Raven into the dense foliage, the smell of smoke still pungent in the air. Dark Star looked back over her shoulder, tears trickling down her cheeks as she clung to her husband. Torn away from her children's resting place, she couldn't bear the overwhelming sorrow.

Brown Sparrow clutched her baby against her heart, hurrying to walk at her friend's side.

"I don't think they plan on killing us!" She ignored Chief Long Knife's scowl in her direction. "Why is Raven leading us? Where are we going?"

"Hush Sparrow," Falcon warned, "Before they change their minds."

"Something isn't right," Chief Long Knife agreed, recognizing most of the warriors as his own men.

They didn't have long to wait before herded toward a clearing. The haunting sound of mourning was the first thing that met them as they were prodded forward.

"Chief," Raven turned, "Follow me."

Chief Long Knife nodded, motioning for his wife to remain outside with the others. Lowering his head he followed Raven into the darkened longhouse, his eyes widening when he saw Kajirowirago and his blond family. A frown lining his forehead, Chief Long Knife stepped forward.

"I am not sure I understand..."

Chief Black Bear struggled to sit up on the pile of furs, Kajirowirago immediately assisting him.

"Welcome to my tribe," the older man coughed, his breathing laboured

.

"I don't have much time left... It is important to me that I have a successor. My wife has not been able to give me children..." Again he paused, his lungs wheezing, "I have heard of you and that you fear the Lord. I have chosen you to lead my tribe when my time comes."

"But you are Mohawk..." Chief Long Knife didn't mask his surprise.

"Yes, but my tribe needs a good leader. As part of the Iroquois Nation, you will be safe..." Dark eyes sought Chief Long Knife willing him to understand - to accept.

"So my people and these Iroquois warriors, turned traitors?"

A low chuckle rumbled the Mohawk chief's chest.

"Do you doubt they would remain loyal?"

The Wyandotte chief chose not to respond as it all became clear to him what had happened. This was an excellent offer. They would have become extinct regardless. Chief Long Knife relaxed the first he was still clenching.

"My people will become Mohawk," his throat constricted, "And I will honour your wife. She will have great respect."

Chief Black Bear motioned for Kajirowirago and the others to assist the Wyandotte in the ritual that would transform them into their most hated enemy - Mohawks.

Chief Long Knife stepped out into the light, his eyes meeting Dark Star's briefly before turning his attention to Falcon.

"The chief does not have long. It looks like the same disease that struck us. I have agreed to succeed him as the new chief but that means we need to become Mohawk."

Falcon blanched.

"It is our only hope."

Chief Long Knife's eyes narrowed as he looked over at Raven - one of the warriors who had betrayed him.

"I'm Kajirowirago," the buff blonde interrupted, "Please, come with us."

He paused, thrusting out his hand.

"We have heard you are a believer in Jesus. It is such a joy to meet you."

Chief Long Knife's eyes widened.

"You're a Believer?"

"Yes. There are quite a few of us who are Christians. Word reached our chief of your faith. He wanted to see you and offer his protection for your tribe but unfortunately..."

Kajirowirago didn't need to say more.

Dark Star reached for Brown Sparrow's hand as Gretjen stepped out of the longhouse, a tender smile on her lips.

"I see you've met my husband. I'm Gretjen and I'm sure you'll meet my sons later - they're the blondes."

A soft whimper escaped Dark Star's lips.

"I'm Brown Sparrow and this is my best friend, Dark Star," Brown Sparrow came to her friend's rescue, cradling her child that much closer to her heart.

Gretjen smiled before looking up at the chief.

"You will be happy here. Come, follow us."

Gretjen led the women away to where other native women stood waiting for them on the river bank.

Turning back to her companions, Gretjen held out her hands.

"May I?"

"Of course," Brown Sparrow nodded, "his name is Eagle...Eagle Isaiah."

"You are just too precious!" Gretjen crooned as the other women reached for the newcomers, assisting them as they became Mohawk women.

For Dark Star and Brown Sparrow, it did not matter to them which tribe they belonged to as long as they were able to live another day with their husbands at their side. Life was far more valuable than tribal feuds.

Stepping out of the river, they were given fresh buckskin dresses, their long hair plaited. The women smiled shyly then stepped back as their chief's wife approached. She was tall for a woman, yet moved gracefully.

When she reached Dark Star, she smiled.

"I am the Chief Black Bear's wife, Fawn. We welcome you into our tribe. When my husband dies, you will take my place..."

Dark Star wasn't certain how to respond, so she reached out and embraced the older woman.

Fawn was startled at the unfamiliar gesture as Dark Star held the older woman in a warm embrace. Her heart went out to Dark Star when she felt an unbidden tear splash onto her shoulder.

Placing her hands on either side of Dark Star's face, Fawn shook her head.

"Do not cry. We will not harm you."

"Oh no, I am not worried about that...I just pray your husband lives. We have suffered such loss, I don't want you to..."

"The Lord gives and the Lord takes away, blessed be the Name of the Lord," Fawn quoted, her voice soft.

Fawn's words were her undoing, Dark Star's tears flowing freely.

"She has lost all her children," Brown Sparrow explained to the women who surrounded them, her voice constricted as she fought tears at her friend's great loss, "All perished except for the child she carries."

Tears pooled in Gretjen's blue eyes before they tumbled down her cheeks. She swiped at them with her sleeve as she passed Eagle back to his mother.

"You and I will be great friends," Gretjen murmured, embracing Dark Star. "We have both suffered great loss and can support each other. Let us go and rejoin our men before they begin to worry."

Fawn was eager to head back to her husband's side, the women following their chief's wife back to the lodge.

Chapter 2

Jaira clung to Strong Oak's neck but had eyes only for Eagle. He shook his head slightly warning her not to say a word as he stepped forward, matching his strides to the warrior who carried Jaira.

"Where are we going?" Eagle frowned.

"To the Mohawk Valley," Strong Oak met Eagle's eyes, "I know you are Iroquois and the Mohawk belongs to your nation. That is why you have been spared."

Eagle bit back a chuckle. Strong Oak was sadly mistaken if he thought he could defeat him. For now, however, he let the matter rest.

"I know Chief Black Bear well. Yes, of course, we will join you. Does he know the Wyandotte have finally been wiped out?"

A shadow passed over Strong Oak's eyes. He was still a member of the tribe that was no more. Once they were assimilated into the Mohawk tribe, they would cease to exist - officially extinct. His stomach clenched, knowing he had played a part in this, but there were no other options. Chief Black Bear was a strong leader who would lead a united tribe to greatness.

Chief Long Knife's life had been spared along with those of his family. There had been no bloodshed of his people. Knowing he had kept his word, Strong Oak straightened his shoulders, adjusting Jaira's weight. His people would live to see another day. Becoming Mohawk wasn't the worst thing that could have befallen them.

JAIRA WAS IN A PICKLE. Now with William long gone, she had time to examine her feelings for Eagle. Unlike the waxy complexioned man she had been married to for over a decade, Eagle exuded virile strength. Jaira lowered her eyes quickly, unable to hide her blush or the tingle spreading quickly down her spine.

Strong Oak shifted her once again, as though aware of the heat emanating from her body, or her treacherous thoughts. Surely he didn't consider them still married? Now that would be a problem.

The sun was low in the sky when they entered the Mohawk village, Strong Oak hesitating for the first time in the clearing. He'd been privy to the plan but was yet to become Mohawk. They'd met in secret in the woods for weeks, but to walk boldly up to the chief he had heard so much about without an invitation...

Eagle noticed Strong Oak's hesitation, but unlike the Wyandotte warrior, he did not miss a beat, stepping forward toward the longhouse where Chief Black Bear would be waiting. A smug grin danced on his firm lips for a moment before disappearing as he announced his arrival.

Strong Oak allowed Jaira to slide down his length, holding her against him as her knees buckled. He stood outside the longhouse uncertain how to proceed. It would be rude to intrude, especially without an invitation.

Jaira held onto Strong Oak's forearm, wishing she were anywhere else. Swallowing hard, she risked a glance up at the man who had once been her husband. Rejecting him may not have been her wisest move as only Eagle and Strong Oak stood between her and an unknown future.

Dark brown eyes with the slightest hint of reddish-gold met her green ones before he looked away, Stong Oak's jaw hardening.

What did she expect? Strong Oak looked like a man scorned and why shouldn't he?

The moments seemed to drag on forever, Jaira's heart hammering in her ears. Glancing up, she expected to see Eagle rejoining them. Instead,

Jaira looked into the impassive, chiselled features of her brother-in-law. It was impossible to say who was more shocked.

"Jaira," Chief Long Knife fixed dark eyes on her, making her squirm in Strong Oak's arms. "We meet again."

Jaira stood with her mouth slightly agape staring at the last man she ever expected to see.

"Long Knife? How?" Jaira stammered, her next thought going to her sister, "Adelaide and the children? Did they survive as well?"

A dark cloud covered Chief Long Knife's features as he looked down without answering Jaira's question. A long silence stretched heavily between them as though the silence could convey all that she had missed since turning her back on her sister and the Wyandotte tribe. He couldn't bring himself to answer Jaira's question.

What felt like an eternity later, Chief Long Knife raised his eyes, their dark depths fathomless as he decided what should be done about her.

"Strong Oak, what are your intentions for this woman? She has already left you once..."

"Can you trust her?" Chief Long Kinfe's words hung unspoken in the air.

"She is mine," Strong Oak replied with a slight shrug of his shoulders as though nothing had transpired between them.

Jaira didn't dare to look up.

"Her husband is no longer a problem," Raven interrupted, a sneer marring his wolfishly handsome features. "I made certain of that."

Jaira muffled a cry, shooting him with a daggered glare.

Unphased, Raven merely laughed in her face but there was no mirth in his laughter.

This was a cruel country and the sooner Jaira realized it, the better off she'd be.

As though no one had spoken, Strong Oak continued.

"She is mine. With your permission, we will stay with the tribe..."

Chief Long Knife swiftly turned his attention from Jaira to Strong Oak.

So there it was.

Could Chief Long Knife forgive the warrior he had once trusted? The fact they were related made the betrayal that much more painful but Strong Oak wasn't exactly offering an apology. In Chief Long Knife's world, Strong Oak was a traitor and his sister-in-law, unfaithful.

They deserved each other.

Without answering, Chief Long Knife motioned with his hand.

"Get them out of my sight."

GRETJEN SAT BESIDE Dark Star in the shadows of the longhouse when Chief Long Knife returned, deep sadness in his eyes. Dark Star met his eyes but didn't say anything as Chief Long Knife turned toward the fire, his shoulders bent.

Fawn left her husband's side, approaching the younger chief.

"What troubles you, Son?"

Chief Long Knife sighed but kept his promise that he would honour Chief Black Bear's wife.

"I am not certain what to do with the warriors who betrayed me and my tribe."

Fawn twisted the tip of her grey-streaked braid, frowning herself. It was true, he was in a predicament.

"Our lives were spared and for that, we owe a great deal to your husband and to God, however, this mutiny was planned for months. If I let it go, then I am a weak leader in their eyes and will have trouble at my door. I will never be able to trust my people and yet..."

Fawn kept her own counsel, waiting for the young man to wrestle with his thoughts uninterrupted. She didn't have long to wait.

"I know God requires I forgive these men and I must obey Him, yet as a leader, I need to show my tribe my strength or it will only summon danger in the future."

Chief Black Bear lay against a pile of furs yet was still able to hear the conversation.

"More than this matter troubles you. Is it that you do not wish to be a Mohawk?"

The old chief had a point. It was rather distasteful that he should lead a people who were his sworn enemies. The Mohawk were known among the native tribes as "Man-Eaters" and a tribe that unleashed fear in any that were not a part of the Iroquois Nation.

Given the choice, Chief Long Knife would rather not have anything to do with this tribe. Instead, he avoided answering that question.

"One of my warriors arrived this evening. He has not acknowledged or apologized for the part he played in this coup. He also brought along a woman and seems to wish to continue as though nothing has changed over the past few months. I told them I do not wish to see their faces right now. I need time to make a decision concerning them. If I ban them from the tribe-"

"-You may win yourself a sworn enemy," Chief Black Bear coughed until bloody saliva dribbled from the corner of his lips.

Fawn discretely wiped away the moisture, preserving her husband's dignity, but her eyes were filled with tears.

Chief Long Knife frowned. He knew he was blessed that the Mohawk chief still held onto life. He wasn't so proud as to not admit he needed training in the ways of the Mohawks or the Iroquois Confederation, but his heart was frosty. Surprisingly, it wasn't the Mohawk people who chilled his heart, but his own treacherous warriors.

"Perhaps it is in your compassion that you will show your greatest strength," Dark Star looked up into her husband's troubled eyes. "In your mercy, you will set yourself apart and win their loyalty."

Chief Long Knife looked at his wife, concealing his surprise. Naturally shy, and especially since the death of her children, Dark Star rarely spoke. His gaze softened as he looked down at the gentle hand she placed on his arm.

"I will deal with this matter in the morning when I have time to pray and sleep on it. Thank you for your wisdom Chief Black Bear and Dark Star." Turning his full attention to his wife, he lowered his voice, "Your sister has returned."

Chapter 3

Jaira looked from Strong Oak to Eagle, then swallowed hard. For the first time in her life, she wished Chief Long Knife hadn't walked away. The irony wasn't lost on her. Just a few months ago she was only too happy to never see him again and yet, right now, at this moment, she wanted nothing more for him to return and rescue her.

Eagle knew this tribe well along with the layout, unlike Strong Oak who stood unmoving, uncertain where to go or what to do.

"Well this is just great," Jaira muttered to herself.

Within a few moments, an elderly woman appeared, a gentle smile softening her weather-worn features.

"Follow me," she motioned with her hand.

Gripping Jaira's wrist, Strong Oak followed Fawn toward a third longhouse that was relatively empty. Fawn looked away from the empty cots, a stark reminder that the angel of death had come to visit.

Smoothing her hand over a few furs, Fawn smiled at Jaira, "You will be comfortable and I will see you in the morning."

Without another word, Fawn turned and left, leaving Jaira in the grip of her husband.

Jaira swallowed hard, fear evident in her eyes. She could have gotten this done and over months ago while she had Adelaide for support, but no, she had been obstinate in her loyalty to William and where had that gotten her?

Strong Oak tilted her chin with a surprisingly gentle finger and a moment later she completely forgot what she had been thinking of.

"We aren't married!" Jaira protested as Strong Oak laid her down onto the soft furs.

"I recall the wedding."

The dim lighting of the longhouse easily hid the humour shining in his eyes.

"I wasn't a willing bride. I recall having no choice in the matter!"

Strong Oak lowered his head, his lips centimetres away from hers. His proximity only served as a hint of what was to come.

Panicking, Jaira struggled against his broad chest.

"I love another!"

"You will grow to love me," Strong Oak was clearly unphased.

"Do your best, but I will *never* love you."

A burst of gentle, rumbling laughter surrounded her.

"You already love me."

Indignant, Jaira's heart beat erratically.

"Pride goeth before..."

Strong Oak didn't let Jaira complete her quote, his mouth claiming what was his.

"MY SISTER IS HERE?" Dark Star stood, immediately turning toward the doorway.

Chief Long Knife placed a tender, yet restraining hand on her wrist.

"Not tonight."

"But... "

"She needs to be alone tonight. You will see her in the morning."

Chief Long Knife's expression made it clear he wasn't to be questioned on the matter.

Dark Star returned to her seat at her husband's side.

"I can't believe my sister returned. How could she have found us?"

"Strong Oak brought her here."

Dark Star's eyes widened.

"He is here? And Jaira? Together?"

Brown Sparrow couldn't hide her giggle.

"True love prevails!"

Dark Star grinned. If that wasn't fate, she didn't know what was.

"My sister was captured by our tribe a few months ago," Dark Star explained to Gretjen who sat with them, her eyebrow arched. "She was given to one of our warriors who had recently become a widower. Strong Oak married her but my sister refused to be his wife - fully."

"Ah," Gretjen nodded, although she still had a lot to learn about the native way of life. "What happened?"

"Well, my sister was still married to William who had been away when she was captured and she refused to...well, anyway, their marriage was dissolved and she returned to Quebec with one of the Jacques, one of the Frenchmen who was working in our village. How Jaira came to be here is a mystery - and with her native husband no less!"

"...And hearing all about it!" Brown Sparrow winked, blushing as she glanced over at her own husband.

"I look forward to meeting your sister," Gretjen smiled warmly, but her thoughts were elsewhere.

Jacque? Could it be one and the same? It wouldn't be surprising if he had been travelling to the Wyandotte tribe. She needed to speak with George - perhaps Chief Long Knife would know more - if Jacques had heard from their son, Harm.

Gretjen was filled with hope, no longer listening to the chatter around her.

JAIRA AWOKE THE NEXT morning before the last stars had disappeared for the night. Slowly exhaling, her relief at not finding Strong Oak still in the bed they had shared was evident.

"Are you hungry?" Strong Oak leaned over the fire he was coaxing to life, not bothering to turn around.

Last night had been less than satisfactory.

Jaira stiffened at the sound of her husband's voice, wrapping her arms around her knees without bothering to reply.

Strong Oak chose to ignore her sullenness, removing the fish from the flames before it burned, the meat white and flaky.

Knowing she was watching him, Strong Oak gestured to the breakfast he had caught not an hour ago.

"If you change your mind," Strong Oak looked away before returning to his own meal.

Finished, he stepped out into dew-drenched dawn - the heralding of a new day. The silence was interrupted only by the sweet songs of nearby birds singing for their Creator. They seemed to not have a care in the world as they tilted their heads, serenading the Heavens.

Leaving his wife behind, Strong stepped away from the longhouse, having more important things to deal with than his wife's sulking.

Jaira waited until she was certain he had left before pushing the furs aside, her eyes on the meal Strong Oak had prepared for her. Remembering all too clearly the corn mush she had been forced to endure a few months ago, the fish smelled heavenly.

Tearing chunks away from the bones, suddenly ravenous, she didn't hear someone enter the longhouse.

"Jaira..."

At the sound of her name, Jaira spun around on her heels, nearly losing her balance.

"Adelaide!"

Her sister smiled but shook her head.

"I'm Dark Star now."

Pressing on as the silence grew awkward, Dark Star continued, "I saw your husband a few minutes ago and thought this was a good time to come see you. I wouldn't want to interrupt anything..."

Jaira turned several shades of crimson as she avoided her sister's gaze.

Humiliating, that's what it was.

"I was so excited when my husband told me you'd returned," Dark Star pressed on quickly, hoping to get past the awkwardness between them.

"Gavin? He's here?"

The colour drained from Dark Star's face at the mention of the husband she would rather forget now.

"No, of course not. I was referring to Chief Long Knife."

Jaira watched a moment as Dark Star involuntarily stroked her extended womb, no longer able to conceal her pregnancy.

"How will you explain this to Gavin?" Jaira's eyes narrowed, "What will he do when he finds out you've been more than a little unfaithful? I can't imagine him being too keen on raising another man's baby."

Dark Star looked away, well aware that Gavin was extremely jealous. What he didn't know...

"Strong Oak is a good man. The sooner you stop fighting your marriage, it will be easier. Trust me, if he's anything like the chief, it will be easy to grow to love him."

"Never!" Jaira scowled, "but I refuse to judge you. What you've done is between you and God, but I will say that I pity you..."

Jaira's thoughts wandered a moment to the all-too-fresh memories of Strong Oak's lovemaking. In truth, it had been more like a waltz of hazy passion than what she had expected - rough, demanding, and taking what he believed to be his right. Jaira would never admit it, even to herself, that it had been wonderful. No, Jaira wasn't a weak woman. She would fight this wrong until it was made right.

Dark Star noticed the soft blush dusting Jaira's cheeks but kept silent.

"Well, I wanted to check in on you and make sure you were alright. We would love to have you join us for dinner tonight. I am sure my husband has invited Strong Oak."

Jaira nodded. It wasn't like she had anywhere else to go and the thought of Adelaide being close by was comforting.

Not that she would ever admit it to her sister.

Chapter 4

Eagle watched as Jaira accompanied her sister to the chief's longhouse. His eyes skimmed over Dark Star. She was slender and tall, carrying herself with confidence, her posture perfect. A hand resting protectively over her round stomach, she didn't resemble her sister much at all.

Jaira seemed to notice his presence, stopping abruptly, and turning in his direction. Her face paled as she looked into his eyes before hanging her head.

A muscle worked in Eagle's jaw as he followed behind the women, joining the others for their evening meal.

Strong Oak sat a short distance from most of the other warriors, as though his shame rooted him on the outskirts of darkness. No one paid him much attention, aware of his part in the treachery that had brought their chief to this tribe. If it wasn't for Strong Oak and their accomplices, they would not have to be the dreaded Mohawk. The disgrace soured on Strong Oak's tongue as his people who weren't involved in the coup turned their backs on him. Strong Oak was well aware he deserved nothing less.

Eagle sat closer to Chief Long Knife and in turn, closer to Jaira who was seated at her sister's side.

"ARE YOU WELL?" BROWN Sparrow struggled to hide her grin as her eyes sought Jaira's. "I hope you are well-rested," she nearly sputtered on her own words, trying to suppress a giggle.

Strong Oak instinctively puffed out his chest as Jaira's head lowered, a crimson stain spreading up her neck until it reached her cheeks.

"I had sufficient rest thank you," Jaira muttered, glancing at Strong Oak beneath lowered lashes.

"You will be staying with the tribe then..." Brown Sparrow leaned forward, her voice hopeful.

"I honestly don't know. I really don't feel like I belong with you guys. I can't be like you - abandoning everything to be like these Indians. For goodness sakes, Adelaide or whatever you call yourself now, you just gave up on everything, even your own husband. Prove me wrong...where are your kids? I bet you don't even know or care. I am not blind, I see you have eyes only for the chief."

Jaira couldn't have known what had happened to the children, but her words were a cruel blow to Dark Star's heart.

Chief Long Knife's eyes narrowed, glaring at Jaira. He hadn't been keen on her since they had first met. He waited a moment for Dark Star to say something, anything, but when she remained silent, only a great, salty tear tumbling down her cheek, he stepped in.

"This is not a conversation I wish to have today. It is distressing for my wife who is near her time. The children of whom you speak were lost in the plague that hit us," he swallowed hard at the sudden lump constricting his throat. "They are with Jesus."

"Oh, Adelaide!" Jaira began, feeling like a fool. "I had no idea. I never would have said... Well, I didn't mean it. Please forgive me..."

Dark Star turned her head away. It was asking too much when her faith was so painfully small.

Baby Wolf fussed a moment before letting out an ear-throbbing howl.

"It is my fault," Brown Sparrow spoke, settling her baby against her heart. "I never intended to cause pain. I was only joking. Shall we start fresh?"

"I'd like that," Dark Star nodded.

Jaira bit her lower lip.

"If we start fresh, does that mean I can be single again?"

She glanced over at Strong Oak who was struggling to mask his emotions. Brave in the face of the enemy, he wasn't nearly as stoic when facing an onslaught of emotions assaulting his heart as Jaira made it abundantly clear before everyone gathered around the fire that she wanted nothing to do with him.

CHIEF BLACK BEAR'S breathing was laboured, his emaciated frame heaving with the struggle to inhale oxygen. His wife knelt by his side, holding Chief Black Bear's frail hand against her tear-dampened cheek. Everyone knew it was only a matter of time before their chief entered the afterlife, yet it didn't make it any easier. No one would wish to watch a man die, and their chief was greatly loved.

Long Knife stood on his other side, fists clenched. The truth was if it wasn't for the dying man's intervention, he'd likely have been the one to enter Heaven's pearly gates first. He owed Chief Black Bear a great debt. With lowered head, Chief Long Knife assured the man before him that as long as he had breath, he would love and lead the Mohawk tribe as though they were his own children.

Chief Black Bear smiled weakly between yet another coughing fit.

"I chose well," he spoke softly with his wife, only increasing her soft sobs.

Long Knife turned away giving the couple privacy in Chief Black Bear's last moments. His spirit was heavy as he stood on the threshold of his new role.

It wasn't as though he didn't know how to be a chief and lead a tribe. Under Chief Black Bear's tutoring, he had learned much about the ways of his new people. On the outside, he now looked as though he had been born a Mohawk warrior. No, the problem ran much deeper than outer appearance.

With the acceptance of Christianity, Long Knife had lost the confidence of many of his people. If the Wyandotte hadn't been so divided...

How did he hope to win the trust and loyalty of a nation that'd been their sworn enemy?

Glancing discreetly over at Raven and Strong Oak who stood together speaking in hushed tones. The now-familiar talons of betrayal dug unrelentingly into Long Knife's heart, twisting mercilessly.

Long Knife's jaw clenched as Chief Black Bear breathed his last.

In a single moment, he was once again, chief.

EAGLE WAITED IN THE shadows, observing the dynamics of the tribe as Chief Black Bear was buried with all the honour a great chief deserved. He didn't know much about the new chief but wasn't about to wait around. The air of unrest in the tribe was tangible.

Waiting until Raven and Strong Oak had stepped out of the longhouse, their voices low, he approached Jaira, lowering his tall frame until he was eye level with the green-eyed young woman.

Eagle's sinewy figure didn't leave any doubt he was a force to be reckoned with if provoked, his dark eyes, lethal. Should any make the unfortunate mistake of betraying him, they wouldn't live long enough to regret it.

Watching Jaira shiver as he invaded her personal space, a sinister expression flickered across his eyes and then was gone before anyone noticed, except for Jaira, that is.

"You never mentioned you had two husbands." Eagle's voice was cold.

"I never intended to lead you on..."

At Eagle's expression of confusion at her choice of words, Jaira continued, "I didn't mean to start anything between us or make you think that there could be something more than friendship." Jaira's cheeks flushed as she avoided looking at the man beside her. "Besides," her voice stammered now, "I didn't think it was important. I didn't expect to see Strong Oak ever again..."

That, at least, was the truth.

Eagle sat in silence, his expression unreadable.

Clearly flustered, Jaira continued to prattle, her voice breathless.

"Now that my husband is dead, I just want to be single. I don't want a man in my life. Romance, for me, is dead."

Again Eagle had no idea what she was talking about.

Romance?

"You belong to Strong Oak. There is nothing for me here," he looked away for a moment, his eyes lingering at the entrance to the longhouse, or the exit depending on how you looked at it.

In one fluid movement, he stood, towering over Jaira.

"You will learn to be happy. At least Strong Oak is not that man you were married to. You deserve better than that weasel."

And with that, Eagle turned his back on her, disappearing from view.

Jaira hugged her chest, a tear tumbling down her cheek.

Chapter 5

Crying wouldn't bring Eagle back. Jaira knew the moment he'd left that if Eagle walked away, she was likely to never see him again. Standing swiftly to her feet, Jaira ran for the longhouse entrance without a second thought.

"Eagle! Eagle!"

Eagle turned towards the woman frantically screaming his name, oblivious to the heavy atmosphere as the tribe mourned the recent loss of their chief.

"Jaira," Eagle frowned, clearly not impressed with the scene she was making.

"You can't leave me here, you just can't!"

Eagle faced Jaira with his hands on his hips, his broad chest gleaming in the late afternoon sun. Jaira's knees buckled, suddenly faint. Eagle wasn't about to fall for feminine wiles. He had seen more than one woman faint on raids.

"You belong here," Eagle lowered his voice as he turned away from Jaira once more, continuing along the path that led to the treeline.

A few more steps and he would disappear from view.

Clutching her skirt in clenched fists, Jaira kept her eyes on Eagle's back, running the short distance that separated them.

"I'm going with you," Jaira said more firmly between gasps for air.

"Jaira! You belong here. Your sister is here. Your *husband...*"

Eagle was unable to hide his emotions in the way he said "husband," the word laced with bitterness.

He had no love for Strong Oak. Yes, he may have been assimilated into the tribe, but in Eagle's world, the warrior was his sworn enemy, his blood Wyandotte. Hatred ran deep - centuries old. The hatred had only intensified now that he knew Strong Oak and Jaira were married. He'd been made to look like a fool.

The truth was, he wasn't sure when he had started to develop feelings for Jaira. Was it when he carried her back to the fort after finding her limping like a battered pup after the Frenchman? The night they had spent together, Jaira clinging to him for warmth? The week he had stayed with her while Brebeuf had been tortured?

Eagle searched his memories for a brief moment, barely aware Jaira had caught up and was clinging to his wrists.

At some point, he had begun to fall in love with Jaira and open his heart to the possibility he could marry her when her husband had been killed. He would woo her, slowly winning her heart. A glimmer of hope for a future together was cut short by the appearance of his enemy who shattered any dream Eagle might have.

There was no disputing the validity of their marriage. Helpless, Eagle had no choice but to turn away, forcing the realization Strong Oak was taking what Eagle wanted more than anything - Jaira. How did Jaira expect him to remain with the tribe?

Eagle narrowed his eyes as he looked down at the woman clinging to him. If things had been different... No, instead he watched her cry, masking his own emotions behind scowling features. He wasn't sure who he should be angrier with, Strong Oak or Jaira.

Jaira.

She had failed to tell him the truth. Strong Oak wasn't to blame. There was no way he would know a spark of love had developed. He was simply being the husband he was entitled to be. Eagle could only hope he would treat Jaira well.

Freeing himself from Jaira's grip, Eagle took a deep breath.

"Jaira, it can never be. You are bound to your husband. I cannot remain here and there is no future for you if you come with me. I will not take you from your husband. To do so would make me dishonourable..."

"I don't care! I'll take the blame," Jaira sobbed, "I love you!"

Eagle stepped back, unable to hide his emotions at her declaration. He bit his tongue - hard - to keep himself from telling her that he loved her as well. Fate had dealt them a bitter blow.

"You belong here with your sister," Eagle began again, frustrated at not being able to keep raw emotion from his voice. "She needs you more than ever. For your sister's sake, you must stay. Give Strong Oak a chance. In time, you may grow to love him..."

Eagle's own words punched him in the gut.

Jaira lowered her head, tears coursing down her fair cheeks.

"Will I ever see you again?"

Eagle couldn't tell her the truth.

"I am sure fate will cause our paths to cross again."

Jaira's shoulders shook with heart-rending sobs.

"Jaira," Eagle tilted her chin, brushing her tears away with his thumb. "Do this for me. Out of the love you have for me, try to accept this new life. Be the brave woman I would want you to be. If it helps, when your husband comes to you, close your eyes and imagine it is me holding you in my arms. You will please your husband and it will be easier for you. If things had been different..."

Jaira didn't care about protocol. She wrapped her arms around his neck, pressing her lips against his.

Eagle tasted her tears for a second before pushing her away. He would not allow himself to be shamed. This tribe had been hospitable and he would not disrespect them now.

Jaira walked slowly back to the longhouse without looking back, rubbing her tear-reddened eyes with her knuckles.

Life was cruel.

STRONG OAK FROWNED as he observed his wife with Eagle. A blind man could notice there was something up with them.

"Are you going to allow your wife to make a fool of you?"

Strong Oak refused to acknowledge Raven's jeer.

"You'll be the laughing stock of the tribe if you don't take matters into your own hands. Jaira's making eyes at that warrior could be seen by everyone. Oh, and he's *Mohawk,*" Raven emphasized the word in case there was any doubt that Jaira's flirting with the enemy wasn't a knife to Strong Oak's heart. Raven wasn't about to let up. "How do you know they haven't been intimate?"

Rage boiled within Strong Oak's brawny chest.

"Enough!"

Raven laughed.

The seed had been sown.

"JAIRA," DARK STAR PLACED a hand on her sister's forearm, gently restraining her. "We clearly need to talk but right now the tribe is grieving. It is neither the time nor the place to be causing a scene. You are bringing disgrace to your husband..."

"Don't even go there, Adelaide! I swear this is *not the time.*"

"In case you haven't noticed, Jaira, we are living among wild people. Think before you react, that is all I'm trying to say. An attempt to fit into the tribe would go a long way. In fact, I'd bet you'll earn more respect than flirting in front of your husband."

"Ah, I see what this is all about now. Let me clarify a little something before you get all high and mighty on me. I didn't get to choose the man I was married off to and I can sure as heck guarantee that it wasn't for love. Unlike you who married at the top of the totem pole going straight for the chief, *I wasn't given a choice.* What did you do? Pick a name out of a hat? Give me someone no one else wants? If he is such a fine husband, why didn't you marry him instead of the chief? Oh right, he was beneath you."

Jaira nearly grinned at her sister's stunned, speechless expression.

"You might want to back off, Addy, I'm still grieving William's death."

If that were true, she wouldn't have been all but falling at Eagle's feet.

Jaira didn't have time to rethink her words as Strong Oak stepped out of the shadows.

"You will not speak to our chief's wife in that manner again."

The tone of his voice assured her she would regret it if she challenged him.

"Right..." Jaira's bitter laughter filled the longhouse. "You are going to tell me how I can speak to my *sister*? It's because of her that I was left behind. Apparently, she needs me..."

Jaira didn't look at Dark Star, now defying Strong Oak with her hands on her hips.

A shadow rested in Strong Oak's eyes.

"If you hate me this much, I will release you from our marriage. Forever."

Emotion strangled his throat. It would have been less painful if she'd never returned.

Chapter 6

The situation between the sisters was escalating quickly on Chief Long Knife's first day as chief. The Mohawk tribe's grief was fresh and raw, emotions high. The timing of this argument was completely wrong.

Gretjen rose from where she had been sitting beside Brown Sparrow cradling baby Eagle. She didn't look at Strong Oak who was struggling to maintain his composure, holding onto his thunderous scowl. His presence was only heightening the tension in the suddenly cramped longhouse.

"Jaira, come with me," Gretjen held out her hand toward the young woman, her voice soothing.

Jaira really didn't have much choice. Where was she to go at this hour? There was no way she would be able to find Eagle now on her own and as for her sister...no, she would rather sit on the opposite end of the longhouse than be anywhere near her sibling.

Following the older woman's lead, Jaira crouched down beside Gretjen, ignoring Brown Sparrow and her whimpering infant. If she could just be left alone...

"Jaira," Gretjen waited until Jaira looked at her before continuing. "I know these changes are difficult for you. I cannot begin to understand how you must be feeling having just lost your husband." Gretjen tenderly stroked Jaira's hand as she spoke. "Are you a Believer in Jesus?"

Jaira nodded, not willing to release her scowl just yet.

"Then you might remember that the Bible says that all things work together for good to those that love God. We might not see it now, but

God is still on the throne and in control. He knows the end from the beginning and is well aware that you are married to Strong Oak. His plan is bigger than what we can see right now."

Gretjen paused for a moment, waiting for her words to sink into Jaira's turbulent thoughts before continuing.

"Whatever our situation, we need to remember God is faithful and will not turn His back on us now."

Jaira's bravado cracked.

"I am not so sure...I feel like my entire life is out of control and I have no say in any of it. I cannot be forced to love that man when my heart loves another. It isn't fair at all!"

Gretjen smiled sympathetically. She knew all about life not being fair. No one had asked her if she was okay with her mother's murder, with her son deserting them, with her husband choosing to live among this tribe without asking her. Without faith, Gretjen had nothing. This, however, was not the time to compare notes on suffering and injustices.

"Give yourself time, and if you ever need to unburden your heart, I'm here for you."

Gretjen's kindness was a ray of light, yet it wasn't enough. Kind words weren't going to bring Eagle back or keep Strong Oak far, far away.

"I am not letting *that man* touch me again," Jaira negotiated her own conditions for her staying with the tribe.

Strong Oak grimaced at the irony of her demands. It was a privilege to stay with the tribe and be offered their protection. She could have a much worse fate than his love. Strong Oak was married to a fool, his own heart still raw from the pain of his first wife's untimely death. Swallowing the lump in his throat, Strong Oak focused on the flames in the middle of the longhouse with unseeing eyes. Chief Long Knife had been wrong in insisting he and his warriors remarry so soon after their wives were barely cold in the ground. Even a warrior can only take so much heartache.

Dark Star crossed the lodge, joining Strong Oak. Her eyes were sympathetic as she placed her slender hand on his arm.

"Jaira is young. In time she may grow to love you."

"I won't beg,"

Turning, Strong Oak left the longhouse.

A CRY OF PAIN ESCAPED Dark Star's lips before she was able to muffle the sound. Chief Long Knife bolted up on the pile of furs they shared, eyes searching the darkness as he reached for the knife he had concealed beneath the furs.

Dark Star dug her fingers into his arm, whether to keep him from charging out of the longhouse after an unseen enemy or from another onslaught of pain, she would never know, but it was effective.

"It's time...please, wake your mother."

Realization dawning, the chief strode quickly to the opposite end of the longhouse. Within moments, not only was his mother awake but Maggie, her mother-in-law, Jaira and Gretjen.

The excitement was tangible as the women prepared to help with the birth of the chief's first baby, Small Bird keeping the secret that this was the chief's second child. The natives who had survived the first raid were very aware of their chief's sorrow, his joy tempered by the realization that should they be attacked again, he could lose this one as well.

Jaira groaned as she moved the furs aside. It would look bad if she was the only woman who remained on her sleeping pallet. Besides, how much sleep would she get with her sister screaming like a banshee?

The men slipped out of the longhouse to await the birth, Chief Long Knife the last to leave, holding Dark Star's hand until the last possible moment.

A twinge of jealousy clenched Jaira's heart as she watched the tender exchange between the couple. She still didn't think much of Adelaide's husband. He was barbaric and Addy still had a husband waiting for her at home. It was wrong no matter what angle you chose to look at it, but their love for each other could not be denied. Theirs was a tender love Jaira could only dream of.

Straightening her shoulders, Jaira joined Gretjen, remaining in her shadow as Dark Star travailed for the next several hours.

Claus poked his head in the entrance, "I'm hungry Mamma."

Gretjen looked up, "I won't be too much longer, son. Please find your father and ask him to get you something to eat."

Claus nodded, his eyes wide as he listened to the screaming reaching his young ears.

"Is she going to live?" His voice trembled with worry.

"Of course," Gretjen smiled, assuring the young child. "There will be a new baby soon. Now, please go find your father or Hans and ask them to get you something to eat. I love you, Claus."

"I love you too Mama," and with that Claus disappeared back into the sunlight.

Gretjen turned back to Dark Star although speaking to Jaira, "Will you please go get some fresh water? It shouldn't be much longer. I'm beginning to see the head."

Jaira stood up, her joints aching from crouching for so long. Blinking against the dazzling sunlight she turned to walk to the river, avoiding the chief's eyes on her.

When he took a step in her direction, Jaira waved her hand as though brushing aside a pesky fly.

"She's fine, don't worry."

"Does she need anything? Is there anything we can do?"

Jaira couldn't help but grin. Gone was the chief's hardened exterior, a vulnerability in his features she had never seen before. At that moment he looked young and at a loss. Just how old was he anyway?

Empathizing with the young father, Jaira balanced the jug of water on her hip.

"Adelaide will be just fine. This baby is her fourth, so she is pretty much a pro at pushing them out by now. You've got nothing to worry about."

Chief Long Knife's eyebrow raised at the mention of Dark Star's English name. It had been so long since he'd heard it.

"Thank you, Jaira."

It wouldn't look proper if he asked her to convey his love to Dark Star. No, he was still chief and the eyes of the tribe were on him. He could never show weakness.

Chapter 7

The labour lasted far longer than Dark Star had remembered with her other children. And the pain...

"One last push," her mother-in-law encouraged her that the end, at last, was in sight.

Within moments the lusty cry of a newborn's protest filled the longhouse bringing smiles to the women surrounding the squirming chief's heir.

"Ah, a boy," Small Bird grinned, kissing her grandson's pudgy cheek. "My son will be pleased."

At that moment Chief Long Knife entered the lodge, his eyes glowing with unmistakable pride.

"Thank you," he murmured, sending his wife a look that spoke volumes.

Dark Star's heart fluttered as she watched her husband reach for their squalling son.

The baby would not have received his name yet according to Wyandotte tradition until his ears had been pierced, but he was not Wyandotte. The child in his arms was Mohawk - the eternal enemy of his people.

Swallowing the tears that burned at the back of his throat, Chief Long Knife raised his son so everyone gathered could see the infant.

"My son, Peter-Torris Hendricks of the Mohawk tribe."

Strong Oak looked away, ashamed of the part he had played in the fate of his tribe. A simple, "I'm sorry," wouldn't change the course of history. The warrior was all too aware that the choices he had made couldn't be reversed. Not now - not ever.

He glanced over at Jaira whose features were as dark as an oncoming storm. Surely the Great Spirit had punished him for sins by bringing Jaira back into his life.

Dark Star, however, was the first to speak.

"Peter...Hendricks? Why that name?"

The name Peter Hendricks that had been given the chief by Brebeuf only stirred memories she'd rather forget. If the chief hadn't shunned the old ways and angered his people...no, that wasn't why her children had died but it was the reason she could never visit their grave. The name broke her heart.

"I owe Brebeuf a debt of gratitude. If it were not for him..."

"You don't know, do you?" Jaira interrupted, unfazed by the chief's position of authority. Not waiting for an answer, Jaira continued. "Brebeuf is dead."

Chief Long Knife's features darkened.

"How do you know this?"

The chief had barely acknowledged Jaira's existence and right now she wished he would continue to ignore her, squirming uncomfortably under his penetrating gaze.

"He was killed. He didn't make it through the week."

Chief Long Knife knew exactly what she was referring to. The tiny man wouldn't have survived the week of brutal torture the Iroquois Nation was notorious for. "Man-Eaters." They thrived on brutality and now he led one of the tribes within the dreaded nation. Chief Long Knife's stomach clenched as he willed his features not to betray him.

Chief Long Knife stepped forward menacingly, passing his son to his wife. He would personally avenge the priest's murder.

Jaira backed up as the chief advanced.

"Tell me!" The chief snarled.

This wasn't the time to play games of cat and mouse.

"Jaira..."

Dark Star was clearly fighting tears over the senseless death of her friend.

For Dark Star's sake, and her alone, Jaira told the truth.

"The Iroquois tortured Brebeuf until he died."

Chief Long Knife emitted a chilling, blood-curdling cry.

"Think this through," Kajirowirago reasoned with the younger man. "You are the chief of the Mohawk now. You cannot battle against your own nation without destroying this confederacy. I can see how much this man meant to you, but you must let it go. In this, your hands are tied."

Chief Long Knife pried his arm away from the tall blonde man, rage clouding his better judgment.

The timing was everything and Chief Long Knife wasn't a fool.

Kajirowirago approached the young chief, a solemnity in his eyes.

"Enjoy the birth of your son, my chief. Your wife needs you by her side now. I know you are a Believer, that is why Chief Black Bear chose you to lead our people. The Bible says *Vengeance is mine, I will repay, sayeth the Lord.*" I never had the privilege to meet Brebeuf, but I can see what a great impact he had on you and your coming to know Christ. Trust me, you do not want to bloody your hands avenging his death. I am certain Brebeuf would not have wanted you to..."

Chief Long Knife knew Kajirowirago was right. He may be German and a foreigner, but the older man spoke with wisdom.

"It is our way," Chief Long Knife wouldn't yield quite yet.

"Was your way..." Kajirowirago softly corrected. "You are a new creature in Christ Jesus. Old things are passed away; behold, all has become new."

Brebeuf and the tall German had an uncanny similarity, spouting off memorized Scripture. Had they met, they surely would have been great friends. Yet what kind of man would Chief Long Knife be if he allowed his friend's senseless murder to go unpunished? Innocent blood had been spilled and a nation looked up to him as their leader. It was his duty to lead them on the warpath or he would look like a spineless fish in their eyes.

At a fork in the road, Chief Long Knife's decision would have long-lasting consequences.

"This is not over," Chief Long Knife held out his hands for his son. "Today we will celebrate the birth of our future chief," his face erupted in a joyous smile.

Just maybe the Scriptures spoke the truth. His new God restored what was taken.

Peter-Torris Hendricks slept, blissfully unaware of the turmoil in his father's spirit or the sorrow in his mother's heart. The future leader of the great Mohawk people suckled his tiny fist, unaware of the legacy resting on his tiny shoulders.

"WOULD YOU LIKE TO HOLD Torris?" Dark Star gently tapped her infant's back, her eyes meeting Jaira's.

Jaira shrugged, turning away.

"Ya, no thanks. I can't wrap my mind around how God chose to give you a child conceived in sin whereas I remain barren. I was married for *years* and yet my womb remains locked up. I don't get it and holding your baby is just a slap in my face."

Dark Star hadn't realized how Jaira was feeling and immediately felt awful.

"I'm so sorry, Jaira, I never meant to flaunt anything in your face or make you feel bad."

Jaira didn't respond. What could she say? At that moment her faith began to waver. Hadn't she been adamant in her fervour for righteousness? Why was she punished with what her heart longed for most while those who lived in sin were rewarded? Something was off and completely unfair. No, she didn't even want to look at her new nephew.

Within a moment, Strong Oak appeared at Jaira's side.

Lowering his voice, Strong Oak cautioned, "The baby is our future chief. Watch your words. Not everyone will be so forgiving, or understanding as your sister."

"I can't express how I feel?" Jaira crossed her arms, but a tear trickled down her ashen cheek. "I've done everything God requires and yet I cannot have a child...life isn't fair."

A tenderness shadowed Strong Oak's eyes.

"I understand your pain. I lost my children to the sickness that came."

Jaira looked at her husband through tear-blurred eyes, their pain something that united them.

Ironic?

Perhaps.

Strong Oak tenderly brushed away Jaira's tears.

"We will have more children."

Jaira lowered her head. He clearly was able to have children. Instead of comforting her, Strong Oak's words only made Jaira feel worse. When he realized it was her womb that was locked up tighter than Fort Knox, how would he feel about her then?

"I can't get pregnant," Jaira hung her head.

A self-assured, sexy grin teased the corners of Strong Oak's lips.

"I am your husband now. We will have a baby."

Jaira blushed crimson, Strong Oak laughing in response. As Strong Oak's laughter enveloped her heart, Jaira would never admit it, but she knew she could have been married off to someone far worse.

Chapter 8

Jaira knew if she was honest with herself, she could fall in love with Strong Oak. After all, he was her husband. Yet, as long as Eagle was out there, she could never give Strong Oak her heart.

Strong Oak, however, had other plans. He'd have Jaira's heart if he could make her forget William and...what was his name? It didn't matter. He had no idea that William was easy enough to forget. Their marriage had been loveless since nearly the first day after they'd signed the marriage license.

Eagle, however, was another matter. He was long gone, but his memory lingered in the shadows of her mind, his wild, untamed scent in the fragrance of the surrounding forest.

Jaira refused to give up hope Eagle would return for her, lifting her in his brawny arms once more. Yes, as long as Eagle was somewhere out there, Jaira could never give in to Strong Oak.

OUTSIDE THE LONGHOUSE, Chief Long Knife stood holding Peter-Torris against his bronze, chiselled chest. His son was pale with satiny hair belying his mixed heritage. Coral streaks laced the darkening sky; a balmy breeze caressing father and son.

In his arms, he held the tribe's future chief. If things had gone according to plan, Peter-Torris would someday lead the Wyandotte tribe. Long Knife's chest clenched in strangled sorrow. He couldn't grieve the loss of his identity - of his people.

Peter-Torris's elder brother should have been chief. Chief Long Knife swallowed hard and then swallowed again. It was the Iroquois Nation who had taken his bride and unborn child and now, with a stroke of bad luck, he was a chief in the same nation that had robbed him of his heart.

Chief Long Knife couldn't keep to himself forever. He would need to meet with the other chiefs sooner than later. Surely they knew where his bride was located.

He may be able to find her now, but then what? What of Dark Star and the babe he now held in his arms? Chief Long Knife was faced with a dilemma. What if Gentle Doe had remarried and was happy? Perhaps she had forgotten him?

No, that was impossible. Surely every time she looked into the child's face she would remember the passion they'd shared - his undying love. What would she think of him now and how quickly he'd remarried?

Gentle Doe would understand that he needed to quickly produce an heir.

A nagging twinge of guilt strangled him. He couldn't pursue this train of thought. Dark Star trusted him with her heart. She'd be justified in feeling betrayed if she knew he still loved his first wife and wanted to find her - even to simply look upon the face of their child just once.

That would never be enough, and he knew it.

Holding Peter-Torris closer, Chief Long Knife vowed no one would take this child from him. He'd learned his lesson the hard way. Never would he leave the women and children unguarded again.

The warriors in his tribe still couldn't be trusted to be loyal. He had realized too late there was a mutiny among his men. Chief Long Knife's faith wasn't as strong as Kajirowirago's. It was only because he didn't trust his own men's loyalty that he didn't avenge Brebeuf's murder. That being said, he wouldn't ever forget.

All in good time...

Peter-Torris wrinkled his nose a moment before emitting a hearty cry.

Masking his raging emotions behind the mask of a warrior's unflinching strength, Chief Long Knife returned to the longhouse.

THERE WAS A STIRRING in the air. It was more than what was visible. In fact, it was that subtle stirring that warned that something was amiss. It was just a matter of time and everyone knew it. It hung in the air - a heavy, unspoken silence.

The young chief stood with legs apart, arms resting across his broad chest. Within moments he would come face to face with his sworn enemies. Yet now, in a stroke of fate, they were his allies and he needed to make nice.

The tribe watched his every move with bated breath knowing what was at stake. Their part in the Iroquois Federation could be revoked. It was crucial they remained as part of the Iroquois Nation. After all, it is better to keep your enemies close, better yet to have them on your side.

Chief Long Knife grimaced. As head of the feared "Man-Eaters," the weight of the world rested on his shoulders.

Chief Red Hawk led the approaching delegates, the other chiefs in the alliance garbed in full regalia.

Dark Star's heart beat a little faster as she watched the line of formidable chiefs, their expressions enough to send a chill straight through one's marrow.

The calm before the storm.

Behind the row of chiefs came what appeared to be warriors. A silent, sure-footed army of men who had been trained from youth not to flinch in the face of torture or death.

Dark Star clutched Torris closer to her heart, her eyes turning back to her husband. It wouldn't be appropriate to hold his hand and offer him support. She would never make her husband look weak - especially not now.

"It will be well," Gretjen murmured, stepping up to Dark Star's side. "He will do well. Besides, I believe like Esther in the Bible, he was brought to this tribe for such a time as this."

"I wish I had your faith," Dark Star admitted with brutal honesty. "Since my children died in the cholera plague, I hate to admit that my faith is not nearly as strong as it was...or may ever be again."

Gretjen gently squeezed the young woman's hand.

"The purest faith is the one born in the fire. Intense pain, I have learned, produces the greatest faith."

JAIRA ASSISTED HER sister and the other women as they prepared and laid out a feast for the visiting chiefs and warriors. A solemnity hung heavily in the air.

Flames danced merrily against the darkened sky, crackling as it licked at the logs. Gretjen averted her eyes, the uncalled-for murder of her mother who met a fiery death at the stake was something that still haunted her dreams.

Some memories are impossible to forget.

Jaira reached for the delicacies Gretjen held in her trembling hands.

"Here, let me help you," Jaira offered the very pregnant blonde.

"Thank you so much," Gretjen smiled her gratitude, not wanting to show vulnerability.

Not now. Not here. Her past was hers and right now there were more important things at stake than memories that refused to release her.

Thankfully, Jaira was distracted. Testosterone was thick in the air, virile warriors watching her every move, or at least that is how it felt. Flushing scarlet, she lowered her head, yet not quick enough.

Penetrating dark eyes met hers, boring into her soul. Her heart skipped a beat. She'd know those eyes anywhere.

Eagle...

He sat on Chief Red Hawk's right hand, his eyes fixed on Jaira. Without a word passing between them, the chief looked over at Jaira and nodded slightly. Jaira ducked her head, set down the platter, and hurried back into the longhouse, nearly bumping into her sister.

"Are you okay, Jaira?"

"Eagle is out there..." Jaira explained, her voice breathless.

"Eagle?" Dark Star frowned, trying to remember who her sibling was referring to. "Ah, now I remember...I wonder what he is doing here."

"I don't know but he is sitting at the chief's side."

Gretjen ran her fingers through her satiny blonde hair.

"He must hold some importance to be seated in a position of prominence...but no matter, you cannot act on your feelings for him. Not tonight, especially. Everything is at stake. One wrong move or perceived slight..."

"I know," Jaira tilted her head, seeking a better view from the entrance.

It was embarrassing to be treated like a child. Then again, the last time she had seen Eagle hadn't been a good scene.

The women watched in silence as the Iroquois chief held out a beaded wampum belt to Chief Long Knife who in turn returned the gesture.

A moment of silence followed.

"We have been informed of Chief Black Bear's death. The disease that came to this tribe did not find us. We welcome you to our federation and have heard you are a man of your word and a great leader."

Chief Long Knife inclined his head indicating that he had heard the compliments, yet his thoughts were elsewhere. Word travelled fast it would seem. Who was the messenger? He was right not to trust his own men. Bringing his thoughts back to the present he realized the visiting chief was waiting for his answer. To what? He'd missed the question.

"I would need to think more about this..." Chief Long Knife stalled, hoping his guest would not realize he had no clue what he had just been asked.

"We do not have much time," Chief Red Hawk leaned back. "I hope to lead my men on the warpath before the new moon. The winter winds will be upon us soon and the French are on our rivers. This is the time to strike."

Chief Long Knife was thankful he had stalled in his answer. He had no quarrel with the French. In fact, the opposite was true. He owed them a debt of gratitude for introducing him to his new God. Without Brebeuf... Chief Long Knife's jaw hardened at the thought. The need to avenge his friend's death still lay beneath the surface.

"My wife was taken from me while I was leading my men on a hunting trip. She was great with child and I was unable to find her or my son after the raid." Chief Long Knife left out the fact it was this man's people who had taken his bride. "My baby with my new wife is not yet seven moons old. I will not leave the women and children unprotected again to fight the French."

Chief Red Hawk frowned. He had expected this new chief to defend the French. It was no secret the man before him was Wyandotte and an ally of the French. His reply, however, was unexpected.

"You lost your wife?" Chief Red Hawk repeated, stroking his jaw. "What was her name?"

Dark Star leaned forward. Chief Long Knife refused to discuss his wife with her...and had never mentioned they had a child together. Talons of jealousy squeezed her heart much too tight.

"Gentle Doe."

Chief Red Hawk searched his memory. Yes, he remembered the beautiful Wyandotte woman who carried a child when they had raided Chief Long Knife's tribe. His wife? Well then...

"I do not know what became of your woman, but yes, I do remember her. She is no longer with our tribe..."

"Where is my wife?" Chief Long Knife's face hardened. "My son?"

"She was traded with another tribe. Gentle Doe was a great beauty and her husband is a widower. He is a good man. Do not fear that she is mistreated. She and your child will be cherished."

"Where is she?" Chief Long Knife repeated, his voice a threatening growl.

A kind husband or not, he couldn't bear the thought this man knew where she was.

"In the south. That is all I know."

Chief Red Hawk studied the young chief with knowing eyes. Would he lead this tribe south on a reckless endeavour to bring back his wife? And to what end? He now had a second wife and baby son. It would only cause trouble and heartache. Was Chief Long Knife a fool after all?

Dark Star met Chief Red Hawk's eyes and looked away, but not before he saw a tear tumble down her cheek.

Chapter 9

"I told you nothing good could come from falling in love with this man," Jaira pointed out, apparently aware of the exchange between the chiefs. "You really didn't think you would get away with being married to two men..."

Dark Star's mortification couldn't have been any greater than to have had a public audience. She had never really wanted to learn the truth about her husband's first wife and especially not like this.

Gavin was the last person on her mind at the moment. She couldn't exactly begrudge Chief Long Knife from having a previous marriage as well. So what bothered her so much then?

The answer was painfully simple. Dark Star's husband loved his first wife far more than she could remember having ever loved Gavin and, unlike Gavin, there was more of a chance of Gentle Doe entering their lives than of Gavin coming to the past - or at least she hoped Gavin never would.

Never before had Dark Star doubted her husband's love, her very future now on shaky ground. Would he leave to find this woman who evidently still held his heart? Dark Star struggled to breathe, the heartache so intense.

Jaira's timing was way off, her words barbed.

Gretjen sighed as she cast a disapproving look at Dark Star's baby sister before intervening.

"Your husband loves you. Trust his heart. He will do what's right."

Dark Star knew Gretjen meant well and sought to comfort her, however, it was impossible to guarantee his love. What if it was an only animalistic desire they had shared all these months? What if her precious Torris was only the result of baser instinct, second-best in his father's eyes?

Only Chief Long Knife knew the answer to her questions - a truth she may never be privy to.

And at that moment Dark Star wished again Arlana had never sent her that accursed necklace.

Unaware of the truth behind Dark Star's predicament, Gretjen led her friend toward the back of the longhouse believing time to herself would be best.

"Feed Little Torris and I'll see to our guests," Gretjen smiled down at the newborn who'd chosen to wail in protest, oblivious to his mother's heartache.

Squatting on the soft pile of furs, Dark Star blinked back tears as she settled her son against her chest. Tears rolled down her freckled cheeks, dampening Torris' downy head. Torris only shrieked yet louder struggling to obtain milk that refused to flow.

Dark Star's shoulders trembled as she cried, unable to hide her sorrow and now she was failing her baby as well. Waves of depression washed over her, constricting her chest in an unrelenting grip.

Chief Long Knife's mother clucked her tongue softly. She'd been unusually quiet, keeping to the shadows since they'd joined the Mohawk tribe. Dark Star didn't question her, believing they were all grieving in their own way those they'd lost in the cholera plague.

"Crying is stopping your milk. This stress is not good. Torris is our future chief. For his sake, you must forget your own sorrow..."

On the surface, Small Bird's words seemed harsh yet Dark Star saw the wisdom behind them. In her arms lay the reason her husband had been quick to remarry. If anything should happen to this baby on her account...

Small Bird wasn't implying their marriage was on shaky ground and was unaware Dark Star had misunderstood her meaning as she retreated further into the shadows.

Dark Star knew her mother-in-law was correct, yet that did not stop the flood of tears. Torris wailed, frustrated his milk supply had significantly dwindled.

Jaira huffed, the sound of the squalling infant grating on her nerves.

"I'm going out for a bit," she said to no one in particular.

"Use wisdom," Gretjen cautioned. "It would be advisable to stay away from Eagle tonight..."

Jaira didn't acknowledge the older woman as she slipped out of the longhouse, stepping into the twilight.

Eagle.

She had never dreamed she would see him again after...

As though reading her thoughts, Eagle looked up, their eyes meeting.

CHIEF LONG KNIFE ENTERED the longhouse long after his guests had departed. The chirping of crickets was the only sound that broke the night's hush.

Dark Star lowered her eyes avoiding her husband's. She wasn't ready to let him see inside her soul. It was better if he didn't know she had overheard their conversation.

Unaware of the strained silence between them or that his wife had overheard his previous conversation, the chief crouched in front of the blazing flames, the flickering light illuminating his taut muscles clenched tight with stress.

Dark Star turned away, gently tapping Torris' narrow back. She needed time to sort through her tangled thoughts.

"Where's my wife?" Strong Oak stepped toward the fire.

Dark Star exchanged a look with Gretjen who had just tucked Claus into the furs for the night.

"I thought she was outside with our guests," Gretjen fixed the stray strands escaping from her tidy chignon. "The last time I saw her, Jaira offered to help serve the food. I naturally assumed she remained with you."

"You are not to blame," Strong Oak lowered his voice attempting to assure the blonde woman who was now fighting tears.

"Could she have gotten lost?" Dark Star's voice was strained.

A dense forest surrounded them from behind, a raging river in front. Wild animals lurked in the shadows and yet her gut knew the truth. Nature wasn't to blame for Jaira's sudden disappearance.

Chief Long Knife stood in one fluid motion, striding toward the door. He didn't say a word as the other men followed him out into the darkness. Tonight they would search for the woman who had never wanted to live amongst them.

Dark Star turned away. If they found her, what then? Would they drag her back kicking and screaming? Jaira was a grown woman certainly old enough to make her own choices and right now, Dark Star was in no position to judge.

It was well past midnight when Chief Long Knife slipped beneath the furs, reaching out to draw Dark Star against his chest. Dark Star instinctively snuggled against his heart before she remembered he'd shattered hers. Pulling out of his arms, she turned away.

Misunderstanding, Chief Long Knife drew her against his side once more before falling into a restless sleep.

"He must love me after all..."

At least Dark Star needed to believe that he did.

BY MORNING IT WAS CLEAR that Jaira wasn't returning home. Strong Oak was nowhere to be seen either, and yet, Chief Long Knife didn't appear to be very concerned. After all, Strong Oak hadn't exactly been loyal and they didn't need traitors in their midst.

Jaira was a grown woman and could make her own decisions and if the traitor decided to follow her to the ends of the earth regardless if she returned his love or not, he was a bigger fool than anyone had estimated, allowing a woman to pull him around by the nose.

Gretjen winced as she watched the others milling about the longhouse. There was different energy this morning. Silence, yet more than that - as though words that needed to be said were being restrained. A stronger pain this time, more like the twisting of a knife burrowed deep within flesh wrenched her gut. There was no ignoring it this time.

"George!"

Her husband turned, startled at the use of his given name. He had been called Kajirowirago for months now, George but a distant memory.

"Gretjen?"

"It's time..."

This little one was a miracle baby, Gretjen on the cusp of not being able to bear children any longer. Claus, she had been certain, was going to be her final child yet this pregnancy was a welcome surprise. Now, as she doubled over as the contractions became more intense and closer together, she wasn't so sure.

The baby seemed as though in a hurry to enter the world and in a matter of a few hours, and one last push, a squirming pink baby boy entered the world, squinting at the smiling faces looking down at him.

Deep blue eyes moistened with tears as he emitted a lusty cry much to his father's delight.

"Another healthy baby boy..." Gretjen looked up into her husband's face.

"Four sons...I couldn't be happier. Do you know how much I love you?" George lowered his voice as though he and Gretjen were the only ones in the longhouse. "You have made me a very happy man."

Chapter 10

Dark Star smiled as she held Gretjen's newborn.

"What will you name him?" She glanced between Gretjen and Kajirowirago.

Kajirowirago looked up from where he stood, flanked by his sons.

"Kajirowirago."

"You can't be serious," Gretjen sighed audibly. "That will be so confusing! Why that name?"

Kajirowirago shrugged with a lopsided grin.

"I like it."

"Then can we go back to calling you, George? It is too much having two of you with the same name..."

Dark Star nodded in agreement.

"You could call him Jr..." She suggested.

Hans rolled his lagoon blue eyes.

"Are we going to go home? What about Harm? Is he coming here?" Gretjen asked as she lowered her eyes.

Her eldest son was still a painful topic.

"He made his choice," Kajirowirago sighed, reaching for his infant son.

"I haven't heard from him since we arrived," Gretjen ran her fingers through her tousled hair. "I worry about him...and if our chief decides to travel south..."

Gretjen's words hung between them as she remembered why Chief Long Knife would choose to leave the valley - to search for his first wife and the child they had together.

"Well, what I mean to say is that Harm has no way of knowing how to reach us."

Chief Long Knife looked over at the blonde woman, her cheeks still flushed from giving birth. He looked startled that she had overheard his thoughts of moving the tribe south. How much more had she heard?

Gretjen and his wife were very close. If she had overheard the entire conversation, well, that would account for his wife's chilly attitude since their guests had arrived. He would speak with Dark Star later...assure her of his love. And yet...Chief Long Knife was well aware of the decision he needed to make.

War was in the wind and their tribe would not be taking part. Not on his watch. Now that little Kajirowirago was here, there was nothing holding them back.

Standing, Chief Long Knife made his announcement.

"Within the next three moons, we will be moving camp. It is time to prepare... We must be on the move before the winter winds arrive."

And without another word, he left the Long House missing Dark Star's sharp gasp.

It looked as though Dark Star's worst fear was about to become a reality. They were about to leave everything behind in search of the woman who still captured her husband's heart.

AS THE TRIBE BEGAN the slow march south, Dark Star held back from her position at the front of the line. Gretjen's older children ran ahead, their blonde hair glistening in the late autumn sunshine. A hint of a chill permeated the air filled with laughter.

The adults walked slower, solemnity replacing the excitement of the youth, yet among those who walked beside her, there was likely no spirit as heavy as hers. A chill laced Dark Star's heart as she watched her husband lead their people to an unknown destination. Each step brought them closer to *her*.

Dark Star had been a fool to give her heart to the chief. Had she been star-struck by his position? Dark Star searched her memories for the moment she had finally learned to love her new husband. This, it would seem, was what she deserved for being unfaithful to Gavin. A better woman would have done everything she could to return home.

What was her excuse? Yes, she had young children...

Dark Star turned her eyes away from her husband's back. If she had run away with the children, just maybe she would have been able to find the portal back to the future...or at least die trying. Dark Star had given up far too easily and...and lost everything.

Torris whimpered in her arms, bringing her back to the present. Well, maybe not everything. She still had Torris, the product of their love.

Dark Star brushed a tender kiss on his dark, silky hair. Yes, Peter Torris filled her once empty arms. A blessing. The memory of his conception made Dark Star blush as she nibbled her lower lip.

Chief Long Knife loved her...he must have...and yet, her mother-in-law implied he had married her to replace his wife and the child they had lost. Dark Star was simply a means to an end - to give him an heir.

Had he ever said he loved her? A tear tumbled down her cheek as Dark Star desperately tried to remember.

Jaira was right. She should have fled with her sister when she had the chance. Instead, she followed her heart only to have it dashed into pieces.

Maybe, just maybe it wasn't too late to go back - to try to find where the little church in the woods had been. Tonight Dark Star would make her move before they travelled too far and she would lose her way.

Tonight Dark Star would do what she should have done months ago...forget all about Chief Long Knife. He belonged where he was - in the past. She needed to get home. Gavin would be waiting and just maybe this was just a bad dream and her children would be by her side once more.

Dark Star had nothing to lose.

IT SEEMED LIKE FOREVER before Chief Long Knife signalled that they would stop for the night. The children who had once been running ahead now dragged their feet beside their parents, rubbing tired eyes.

The women worked quickly preparing a small meal, the flames of the cooking fires snapping against the darkening sky. With her head lowered so their eyes wouldn't meet, Dark Star served her husband then turned away quickly before she could rethink her plan.

"It's for the best for both of us. He will forget me once he finds her anyway. He can't have two wives, so I'm actually doing him a favour."

Retreating into the shadows, Dark Star separated her meagre belongings from his, packing just enough for her and the baby.

Torris...how would she explain him to Gavin? Gavin would be livid if she returned with another man's baby. Dark Star couldn't exactly leave him behind either. Torris would never survive without his mother, and she couldn't have his needless death upon her conscience.

Should she speak with Gretjen? Ask her friend to be a wet nurse?

No, that wasn't a good idea. Her husband couldn't be trusted, at least not that she could see. If she told Gretjen and her husband found out, Chief Long Knife would be notified - it was almost a given.

Dark Star had no choice. She'd have to leave with the chief's heir and face Gavin's wrath. Dark Star swallowed hard.

If only...

DARK STAR FLINCHED as her husband draped his muscled arm across her ribs, pulling her closer to his side. His scent was heady - intoxicatingly masculine. Ignoring her rapid heartbeat, she waited until his breathing grew heavy before inching away from his embrace. Dark Star's eyes traced the outline of his silhouette before stepping away from the furs that served as a bed.

Why was she torturing herself?

He had never truly loved her or he wouldn't be leading the tribe on a quest to find his one true love. She would be a fool to stay with him only to be humiliated in front of the entire tribe when he found the one who held his heart.

Torris.

Would this other woman accept the baby as her own? Her own child would be chief instead, not the babe innocently suckling his fist. Torris would have no future in his father's new family. A fate no better than the Biblical Ishmael, Dark Star could only presume.

That settled the matter. After all, Dark Star had lost everything - her children lying in an unmarked grave. Without Torris, she would have nothing. The chief, on the other hand, was about to find his long-lost child.

Hushing her baby, Dark Star held him to her breast to muffle any sound that might give her away, and, without a backward glance, slipped into the night.

Chapter 11

Gretjen sat in a far corner of the makeshift camp, her boys fast asleep on their mats at her side. Her husband had stayed up late speaking with the warriors in hushed tones then returned without saying a word to explain why a frown etched his brow. Kissing his sons' heads, he led his family in prayer before turning to his own sleeping mat. Gretjen knew her husband enough to know something was wrong, but she wasn't one to pry.

A movement in the darkness caught her attention as she raised her infant to her shoulder, rubbing his tiny back.

Dark Star.

Gretjen watched for a moment as the younger woman slipped out of the entrance without a backward glance, clutching her baby. Something wasn't right.

Without making a sound, Gretjen followed her into the darkness, well aware of the dangers lurking in the surrounding forest. What was Dark Star thinking, leaving the safety of their camp?

"Dark Star," Gretjen called out, her long legs quickly making up the distance between them.

The younger woman looked back with a start, her face ashen in the moonlight.

"Oh Gretjen, I thought you were sleeping," Dark Star bit her lower lip but didn't say any more, averting her eyes.

"It's dangerous being out alone at this hour..." Gretjen reached out, placing a hand firmly on her friend's forearm. "Talk to me."

"No, Gretjen, you've been a friend to me over these past weeks, but the less you know, the better. Please, I need to do this."

"So the chief doesn't know..." Gretjen's voice was low as she expressed what was becoming more clear by the moment. "But why? You won't make it far alone Dark Star..."

"I'm not Dark Star. I'm Adelaide," wincing at the name which now sounded so foreign on her own tongue.

"Are you trying to find your sister?" Gretjen refused to let the matter rest. "I'm sure if you speak with your husband, he will send some warriors out to search for her. Perhaps they will bring her back. There must be a better solution than you disappearing into the night. Dark...I mean, Adelaide, this is foolishness. You won't survive and abandoning your husband will devastate him. Taking his child... Have you thought this through?"

"Please, this is hard enough. I've thought of everything you have said, but no, I need to do this and before the tribe wakes. I need to be long gone by sunrise."

"I know you love Jaira, but Adelaide, you are the chief's wife. You cannot leave like this. Your sister may come to her senses..."

"Gretjen, I know you mean well, but it is Jaira that is correct. In fact, she was right all along. It was a sin for me to marry Long Knife..."

"I don't understand..."

"I am married to another. It is so hard to explain, but my first husband, Gavin, is likely worried sick about me. If I had tried to go back to him when first captured, I'd still have my children."

A sob caught in Adelaide's throat even as she spoke the lie. Theirs hadn't been a great marriage. Long Knife treated her like a queen in comparison, but sin was still sin. She would have to return to her loveless marriage and then, just maybe, God would forgive her for what she had done.

Gretjen embraced Adelaide with her free arm.

"Let me walk with you for a bit then. You know you can always talk with me - share your heart, don't you?"

The kind words were Adelaide's undoing, silvery moonbeams illuminating Adelaide's tear-streaked face.

"I need to find my husband. The chief is looking for his first wife and will be happy once he finds her. There is no place for this baby and I in that future. Don't you understand?

Had I not married the chief but run away and looked for my husband, I would still have my children. It rips my heart out every time I see your boys, and now this... I can't bear it, Gretjen. I had thought to leave Torris with you. After all, you could see to his needs, but what would he be to his father once the first child is found - the rightful heir?

No, my son cannot be an Ishmael in his father's eyes. My children are gone. God, in His mercy, has given me another child to hold in my arms..."

Gretjen dabbed tears spilling from her own eyes as she listened to her friend's heart. What, really, could she say?

"Brown Sparrow will be devastated if you leave without saying goodbye. She has told me you are all she has left of her former life before the raid. You are not alone - Brown Sparrow and I are here for you.

I understand what you are saying about your husband. I don't really know what to say. How God allows such things to happen to those who love him... A test, perhaps, to see if we will still love Him even if all is taken from us?

Please, Adelaide, reconsider. Come back to the camp with me and in the morning, I will ask my husband to see if someone can be sent to look for your first husband. They can be discreet and besides, I need to send a message to my son in Germany as well."

In the distance a wolf howled, sending shivers down Adelaide's spine. She wouldn't be able to find her way in the darkness and the creatures lurking in the forest were undoubtedly hungry.

"Chief Long Knife can't know any of this - or his mother. Your husband would have to be very discreet."

Gretjen nodded as they turned back to where the tribe lay sleeping.

"I am not promising to stay," Adelaide lowered her voice as they approached the shelter, "but it would be easier if he could be found first…"

Nothing more needed to be said. The women embraced once more before returning to their own sleeping quarters.

Chief Long Knife stirred in his sleep as Adelaide slipped beneath the furs, resting his forehead on the back of her neck. Adelaide blinked back fresh tears. She'd miss being held in his arms.

"IS EVERYTHING ALRIGHT my Love?" A hoarse whisper shattered the complete silence of the night.

"Yes, George, I am fine. We will speak more in the morning."

"I am here. Share your heart with me. You will sleep better afterward. Are you worried about Harm? I have noticed he has not written and now that we are on the move, I am not sure how we will receive word from him. Are you homesick?"

His words, though tender, tore at her heart. George knew her better than anyone. The restless nights worried about her firstborn and never hearing from him tore at her heart. It had been months, surely it did not take so long to send word.

"Why are we here George? I cannot help but think our presence isn't needed. Our children should be at home continuing their education. They will need to provide for their families someday and since we have left Germany, we have only suffered loss. I can't help but wonder if we sought God's will as much as we ought to have or was this something we chose to do based merely on emotion - a longing for adventure in our later years."

Gretjen's words were solemn, yet George chuckled.

"We are not that old as you seem to imply by 'Our later years.'" Reaching out, George tenderly stroked his namesake's golden hair. "No, it would seem that life is just beginning. I believe we are here for a purpose. These precious people have never heard the truth of the Gospel - that salvation is found only through the death of Jesus Christ and in faith in His sacrifice. This man that brought the Gospel to them was sadly mistaken and well, when the time is right, I will share with the men the truth. Their souls depend on it."

Gretjen nodded. The truth was, she and her husband had not had much time alone since he had changed his name and became one of the natives. At the time, she really didn't understand but respected his decision.

"You believe they will trust you more if you are one of them?"

"I don't know, Gretjen, but it is more than that. I have spent so many years on the battlefield fighting for something that in the end didn't matter all that much. So many lives were lost. I am deeply troubled that Harm decided to stay behind. I can only hope that when this young love has passed, he will join us out here. It truly is God's Country. I have to believe we have been given a second chance. No, rather, I have been given another chance to make a difference. Can you understand?"

Gretjen wasn't sure if George could see her nodding in the darkness or not. Regardless, George continued.

"I have never felt so alive since we have come to this land. Yes, we have faced death. Yes, I miss my eldest son, but here - I can't even put it into words - here, the door is wide open, and life matters. Every moment, life matters...and yet, here we do not need to fear that our neighbours will betray us if they catch us praying. We have no reason to fear that our children may one day suffer the same fate as..."

George cut his words off short. Bringing up the horrific manner in which Gretjen's mother had died for her faith was something he had never done before now. He instantly regretted his words.

"I'm sorry...I didn't mean to open a raw wound."

Gretjen reached out and placed her hand on George's finely chiselled jaw.

"You have not caused more pain, My Dear, it is well. Thank you for sharing your heart with me tonight. I understand, I truly do, although I am not sure God's purpose for me quite yet. I am not nearly as assured as you are that this is where God wants me to be."

"Have faith, Sweetheart. I love you dearly and thank you for trusting me and remaining at my side."

Gretjen smiled in the darkness a moment before feeling her husband's lips claim hers. Their kiss was tender, lingering - a silent promise between the German couple. Sighing, Gretjen clung to her husband as he pulled her closer to his chest.

"George..." She breathed before her husband drifted off to sleep, content to hold his wife. "Do you think you could discreetly ask what has become of Jaira? I worry about Dark Star. She seems so sad and I wish I could help more. I am trying to encourage her, but other than offering words of support, my hands are tied. Would you be able to help without alerting the chief's attention?"

"Chief Long Knife is her husband. If something is amiss, he shouldn't be left in the dark," George's voice was low as he struggled against sleep.

Dawn was approaching, the first birds bursting into song.

"Of course, I don't mean that we should betray the chief. I just think that he will be more at ease if Dark Star is happier and he does not need to worry about her. If we can find out about Jaira for her, then it will take that burden off her shoulders and she will be in a better frame of mind for the baby as well."

"Alright, I will see what I can find out but if more becomes of this we cannot keep it from our chief. I will not betray his trust..."

Gretjen knew he was referring to their earlier conversation.

"Of course. Goodnight...and thank you."

"Anything for you, My Dear. I am one very blessed man."

And with that, they fell asleep as the sun began to rise over the hills.

Chapter 12

By morning George was once again Kajirowirago as he sat among the warriors, his lagoon blue eyes fixed on the wooden dish containing steaming corn mash. The children had already eaten and now were restless, eager to move camp.

Kajirowirago glanced over at his wife who sat with Dark Star, the women speaking so softly the men couldn't hear a word of their conversation. Perhaps it was for the best. He felt guilty for going behind his chief's back yet there seemed to be no other alternative. Kajirowirago was caught between a rock and a hard place.

"My chief, I was wondering about Strong Oak. Have you heard from him since…?" Kajirowirago allowed his words to hang in the silence a moment before continuing. "My wife is troubled that Jaira has left and now that we are moving camp, may not find her way back. I was thinking by now Strong Oak may have located her and wondered if you had heard from him."

Kajirowirago didn't meet Chief Long Knife's smouldering gaze, already knowing this was a sensitive topic. He was not yet over the betrayal of his people months ago. Strong Oak was the last person on his mind. Without waiting for an answer, Kajirowirago continued. He could blame his lack of understanding of tradition. After all, he was still a German by birth.

"Could one of your men be sent to search for them? Or at least to let them know how to find us should they choose to come back?"

"They've made their decision long ago. It was always in their hearts to break faith."

"And yet, with winter coming, Jaira may miss her sister and regret her actions. She is only a young woman after all and Gretjen has told me she lost her husband in the raid. Excuse me if I am misstepping here, but in her grief and youth, I believe she is making rash decisions she will come to regret."

Gretjen had noticed the change in the men's conversation and laid a hand on Dark Star's arm as they listened for their chief's answer. If they found Jaira, would they not find Dark Star's first husband? Isn't that where Jaira would have headed to? Home?

Chief Long Knife set his dish to the side and stood in one fluid motion.

"Yes, she is young and will need her sister. Black Crow and Calling Bird, search for Jaira and see if she will return to the tribe. As for Strong Oak, do not speak his name to me again. He had been given a second chance and yet never showed remorse but slipped away in the night like a coward after a woman who did not return his love. He is weak and a traitor."

No one argued the point. It was true. Strong Oak would only weaken the tribe and could not be counted on. With a nod from their chief, the two young warriors slipped away into the crisp morning air.

"How will they know where to find us if we move camp?" Kajirowirago asked as he joined the others preparing to leave.

Crow's Wings grinned, his honey-brown eyes, mirthful.

"They are two of our best scouts. No one can hide from them, least of all an entire tribe moving as slowly as a frozen river."

Kajirowirago couldn't help but chuckle at that very accurate description.

"You have a point," he grinned, "how long do you think it will take us to reach our destination?"

Dark Star gasped, holding her breath.

The older man shook his head.

"We need to move slowly because of the babies and their mothers, but at the same time, we need to arrive before the snow comes."

Dark Star didn't have much time.

THE THREE FRIENDS WALKED side by side, Brown Sparrow clutching her toddler's pudgy hand as he tugged pointing at Gretjen's older boys.

"Oh Isaiah, you'll be grown soon enough!" Brown Sparrow laughed at her headstrong son.

Dark Star was too distracted to smile.

"Even if they find Jaira, it will not make a difference."

Brown Sparrow raised her eyebrow oblivious to the midnight meeting the night before or the men's conversation earlier that morning.

"Jaira was miserable with us..." Brown Sparrow began.

"I know," Gretjen nodded, adjusting her baby. An empty sling hung on her back, her restless baby nestled close to her heart. "I just couldn't think of another way to get George to find a way to get someone to look for Adelaide's first husband. I assume if they find Jaira, they will find him as well..."

Brown Sparrow looked from Gretjen to Adelaide and back again.

"Am I missing something? Never mind, clearly I am. What husband? You never mentioned him before..."

"No, and I'm sorry. It is not that I didn't trust you," Adelaide quickly assured her friend. "It is just that I was confused and ashamed and..."

"So that is why it took you so long to..." Brown Sparrow's words hung as she remembered how much Adelaide had resisted any intimacy with the chief, married or not.

Now it all made sense.

Unlike Brown Sparrow who had been unable to shake the nagging feeling that her own husband had passed away when he did not return for her, Adelaide had resisted, even planned an escape.

Glancing over at Falcon, she hadn't made a mistake. He was truly wonderful, she and her child cherished. The swell beneath her soft buckskin dress rippled, choosing that moment to remind his mother she had made the best decision and the passion she and Falcon shared would ensure her arms and heart would never be empty.

"....will never head that way!"

Brown Sparrow shook her head. She had missed the entire conversation.

"JAIRA DIDN'T COME HERE with me in the first place so I have no idea where she is going. We live four hours away from each other by car!"

When both her companions looked at her as though she were speaking another language, Adelaide realized her mistake.

How could they understand?

These women belonged in the past, Adelaide alone to the future.

Adelaide shook her head.

"I fear the men were sent on a wild goose chase and I am no closer to returning to my husband than I was yesterday."

Dark Star gasped at Adelaide's words.

"You can't mean it! You can't seriously want to leave our chief after all this time and return to your first husband?! Especially when this other man hasn't even tried to find you!"

"What if he couldn't?" Adelaide mused aloud, speaking more to herself than to anyone else.

Adelaide nibbled her lower lip remembering all too well details of her marriage she had no intention of sharing with her friends. There was every chance that even if he could have found a way through some magical time portal, Gavin would have moved on with his life. That wasn't the issue. It was up to Adelaide to do the right thing whether or not Gavin was waiting for her with open arms.

"And have you thought of Torris? You will destroy your husband if you take his son from him." Brown Sparrow was frowning, yet empathized with Adelaide's dilemma.

What would she do if Guillaume had been looking for her all this time when she had assumed he had died? Would she turn to her first husband leaving Falcon behind and take their unborn child with her?

The thought made her blanch and knees buckle.

Gretjen reached out instinctively to steady the slender brunette.

"I think you need to tell him the truth," Brown Sparrow rested her hand on her protruding stomach. "He deserves to know everything and there is no doubt he is wise and fair. It is much better to tell the truth in this matter than run off and cause him to worry, let alone break his heart. Your husband is responsible for the entire tribe. This decision, if you make the wrong one, will affect all of us."

Adelaide didn't say a word, averting her eyes as though afraid Brown Sparrow could see into her soul. It was more complicated than being married to two men. Chief Long Knife may be wise, and no, she wasn't questioning his wisdom or leadership skills...it was a matter of his heart.

Could he make the right decision when his heart belonged to another?

Hardly.

"I guess we will have to wait and see if the men are able to find my sister." Adelaide shrugged, hoping to signal she wanted the conversation to come to an end.

Gretjen shook her head.

"They haven't been gone long. If you speak to the chief now, he can put an end to their quest. I don't know what lies ahead, but we should have all able-bodied men with us. If this isn't about Jaira, and clearly it isn't, then they need to be summoned back, I should think..."

Before Adelaide could respond, Gretjen signalled for Hans to join them.

"Hans, go to your father and ask him to get the chief to wait. It is important."

Hans was fast and darted off without a moment's hesitation and within moments the entire tribe came to a standstill.

Chief Long Knife turned to Adelaide with concerned, questioning eyes.

Ready or not, it was now or never. Swallowing the lump in her throat, she walked toward the chief, her eyes fixed on the hand he held out to her.

And the tribe waited.

Chapter 13

"**A**re you alright? Our son?"

Looking down at the peaceful features of his heir, Chief Long Knife returned his focus to Adelaide.

"We can go slower if it is too much for you."

Slower would be perfect - or even better if they turned around and forgot all about travelling to reunite him with his long-lost love.

Adelaide decided to keep her thoughts to herself.

"I am worried about the men you sent out today. It was kind of you to think of my sister's well-being, however, this is the second time she has left the tribe of her own accord. Jaira is not happy among us and knows the dangers out there but chose to take the risk rather than remain with us. I believe it would be better for the men to return so they can help those who are here - who trust you and your leadership, unlike my sister."

A hint of a smile tugged at the corner of the chief's lips.

"So you stopped the entire tribe out of concern for my scouts? You truly have a heart for my people. Come, we will continue and you will walk by my side. We have not had much time together over the past few weeks..."

Adelaide looked up in shock. He was very good at playing the part of a devoted husband. Of course, he couldn't show up rusty, and who better to practice on than the mother of his child?

Keeping her mouth shut, Adelaide simply fell into step beside the tall warrior, listening as he instructed another warrior to fetch the scouts he had sent out mere hours before. Was he embarrassed to have changed his mind in front of those who looked up to him?

Chief Long Knife's face was unreadable.

"Something else troubles you," Chief Long Knife turned, observing her intently studying his features.

They hadn't spoken much since he assumed the role of Mohawk chief, something both knew he never wished for himself. The strain of the past few weeks lingered in shadows haunting his brown eyes, but right now, his entire concern was for Adelaide.

"Why are we going south? Why are you moving the entire tribe and what is the rush to arrive before the snow comes?"

Taken aback, Chief Long Knife looked away and in the fleeting moment when he turned his face from her, Adelaide had all the answers she needed.

"It's okay..." Adelaide croaked, her voice catching in her throat, constricted with unshed tears. "Forget I asked."

And with that, she stepped backward, blending into the crowd that was steadily stepping forward towards Adelaide's nightmare and farther from her children she had left behind.

Taking a deep breath, it was now or never.

Without a word, Adelaide watched in silence as the tribe she had lived amongst for months milled past her. She wasn't as close to Small Bird as Brown Sparrow was to her mother-in-law and at this moment, Adelaide thought that might be for the better.

One less tearful goodbye.

When the last of the women had passed her, Adelaide sprinted towards the forest, clutching Torris to her heart. She needed to make up for lost time, and there wasn't a moment to waste.

THE SUN WAS BEGINNING to set when the tribe stopped once again to set up camp for the night. Chief Long Knife glanced up at the orange-streaked sky, sighing heavily before turning toward the small campfire.

Hunching down, Chief Long Knife stretched his palms toward the crackling flames, his thoughts distant. If he were honest, he wished they were making better time, but it could not be helped. He would not risk any harm coming to the infants or their mothers. Speaking of which...

Chief Long Knife turned his gaze from the flames, looking among the women milling about preparing the evening meal for a glimpse of his wife. She must be taking care of Torris he surmised before turning to the tall blonde who was seeking to gain his attention.

Not needing an invitation, Kajirowirago lowered his voice.

"My wife is concerned that our son who remained in Germany will not be able to write to her. We have been waiting for months for a letter and there has been nothing yet. I would like to assure her that she would still be able to receive word from our son should he write, but I am not even aware of where we are going or how to send word to him that we have moved."

Chief Long Knife didn't say a word. He knew all too well what it felt like to love someone and never hear from them again.

"At the pace we are moving, it will take longer to reach our destination than I had anticipated."

"I am not questioning your leadership..." Kajirowirago quickly explained.

Again the chief was silent, lost in his own thoughts.

"We must put as much distance between us and the Mohawk Valley as possible before the new moon. That is my greatest concern. I believe there is a fort near where we are headed. We will stop and you can send word to your son. It will be well."

Chief Long Knife's throat tightened even as he said those words. He wasn't certain if they were walking into hostile territory. Perhaps before when he had been Wyandotte, but now as leader of the feared Mohawk tribe, he could only hope things would be different and the white man would be an ally.

He didn't have much time to contemplate the situation when Gretjen ran toward where they were seated, her features ashen.

"Dark Star," she gasped, "Dark Star is gone. I didn't think she would actually do it after…" Gretjen quickly looked away.

Chief Long Knife leaped to his feet.

"She has gone after her sister…" He muttered before turning away then stopped, mid-stride. "No, I cannot go after her. I must lead my people."

Chief Long Knife looked between Falcon and Kajirowirago, the two men he trusted most - the only two who had never betrayed him, at least not yet.

And yet…no, he could not ask them to leave their wives when the women were most vulnerable. Chief Long Knife remembered all too well what had happened when he had left his very pregnant bride - a decision that haunted him every single day. He, on the other hand, could not trust his wife and infant son with any of the others. In his eyes, they were either traitors or ruthless savages he had no choice but to lead. Sometimes, one simply had no choice over their destiny. If they did…he certainly would never have chosen to be the leader of the Mohawk tribe. Almost anything would have been a better fate.

Kajirowirago watched the shadows flicker across their chief's features as he wrestled with his duties as a husband and a leader of a tribe.

"Send word to my scouts. Tell them they must return as quickly as possible and find my wife and son. Jaira is the least of my concern right now."

Falcon nodded then retreated to relay the message to the men in question wondering why he had not been chosen to find Dark Star and bring the chief's family back.

Dear Reader,

I hope you enjoyed this 3d book in the series. Please leave a review - it would mean the world to me.

If you have an account on Goodreads, please consider following me - I follow back :)

You can also find my VIP reader group on Facebook and on Gab called:

Novels by Angeline Gallant: Fan Group

Thank you once again for your support,

~ Angeline ~

Don't miss out!

Visit the website below and you can sign up to receive emails whenever Angeline Gallant publishes a new book. There's no charge and no obligation.

https://books2read.com/r/B-A-QGSI-IRSTB

BOOKS 2 READ

Connecting independent readers to independent writers.

Also by Angeline Gallant

Calling Her Heart
No Turning Back
Calling Her Heart volumes 3 & 4

Keeper Of Secrets
A Lady's Secret

Midnight's Awakening
Kyralie
An Alpha's Princess
Midnight's Awakening boxed set volumes 1-3

Secrets of the Underworld
Secrets of the Underworld Volumes 1 & 2

Tell My Story Collection
Tell My Story: Germany 1851

Tell My Story: England 1852

The Grave Whisperer
German Prisoners of War in Canada

The Wolf Whisperer Series
The Cry of the Wolf
Captured Heart
Journey of the Heart
Fate's Legacy
Mohawk Valley

Standalone
Remembering Volga Germans: A Handbook for Authors and
Genealogists

Watch for more at https://www.goodreads.com/author/show/
19703964.Angeline_Gallant.

About the Author

Angeline Gallant is a Geneology addict who loves to work on her family tree and help others with theirs. This passion for history plays a huge role in her books as well. She's an avid reader and writer of historical fiction and she can even sometimes be found in cemeteries recording information and working on historical projects in her spare time.

An Old Stock Canadian and a homeschooling mother living in Canada, Angeline is determined to leave her own special mark on the world through her work, her child, and her writing.

It is her hope to inspire others to learn more about their histories and the history of the people that have come before us.

Angeline is an author on Goodreads. If you follow her account on Goodreads, she will follow back.

Read more at https://www.goodreads.com/author/show/19703964.Angeline_Gallant.